A NOTE TO PARENTS

Reading Aloud with Your Child

Research shows that reading books aloud is the single most valuable support parents can provide in helping children learn to read.

- Be a ham! The more enthusiasm you display, the more your child will enjoy the book.
- Run your finger underneath the words as you read to signal that the print carries the story.
- Leave time for examining the illustrations more closely; encourage your child to find things in the pictures.
- Invite your youngster to join in whenever there's a repeated phrase in the text.
- Link up events in the book with similar events in your child's life.
- If your child asks a question, stop and answer it. The book can be a means to learning more about your child's thoughts.

Listening to Your Child Read Aloud

The support of your attention and praise is absolutely crucial to your child's continuing efforts to learn to read.

- If your child is learning to read and asks for a word, give it immediately so that the meaning of the story is not interrupted. DO NOT ask your child to sound out the word.
- On the other hand, if your child initiates the act of sounding out, don't intervene.
- If your child is reading along and makes what is called a miscue, listen for the sense of the miscue. If the word "road" is substituted for the word "street," for instance, no meaning is lost. Don't stop the reading for a correction.
- If the miscue makes no sense (for example, "horse" for "house"), ask your child to reread the sentence because you're not sure you understand what's just been read.
- Above all else, enjoy your child's growing command of print and make sure you give lots of praise. *You are your child's first teacher—and the most important one. Praise from you is critical for further risk-taking and learning.*

— Priscilla Lynch
Ph.D., New York University
Educational Consultant

For Winnie
—J.S.

Text copyright © 1996 by Jeffrey Scherer.
Illustrations copyright © 1996 by Jeffrey Scherer.
All rights reserved. Published by Scholastic Inc.
HELLO READER!, CARTWHEEL BOOKS, and the CARTWHEEL BOOKS logo
are registered trademarks of Scholastic Inc.

Library of Congress Cataloging-in-Publication Data

Scherer, Jeffrey.
    One snowy day / written and illustrated by Jeffrey Scherer.
        p.   cm.—(Hello reader! Level 1)
    Summary: A group of animals get together to build a snowman.
    ISBN 0-590-74240-X
    [1. Animals—Fiction. 2. Snowmen—Fiction.] I. Title.
    II. Series.
    PZ7.S346670n   1996
    [E]—dc20   95-30066
                                                                CIP
                                                                 AC

12 11 10 9 8 7 6 5 4 3 2 1   6 7 8 9/9 0 1/0
                    Printed in the U.S.A.   24

First Scholastic printing, December 1996

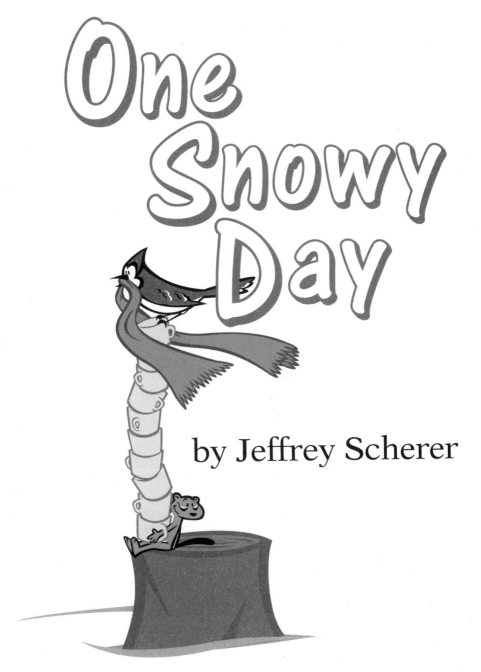

One Snowy Day

by Jeffrey Scherer

Hello Reader! — Level 1

Cartwheel BOOKS®

SCHOLASTIC INC.
New York Toronto London Auckland Sydney

Bear picked up
the branches.

Deer brought the broom.

Mouse
borrowed
the buttons.

Blue Jay
flew in
the scarf.

Kitten
found the
mittens.

Squirrel carried
the acorns.

Rabbit
gave up
a carrot.

Skunk offered the hat.

Chipmunk
juggled
the cups.

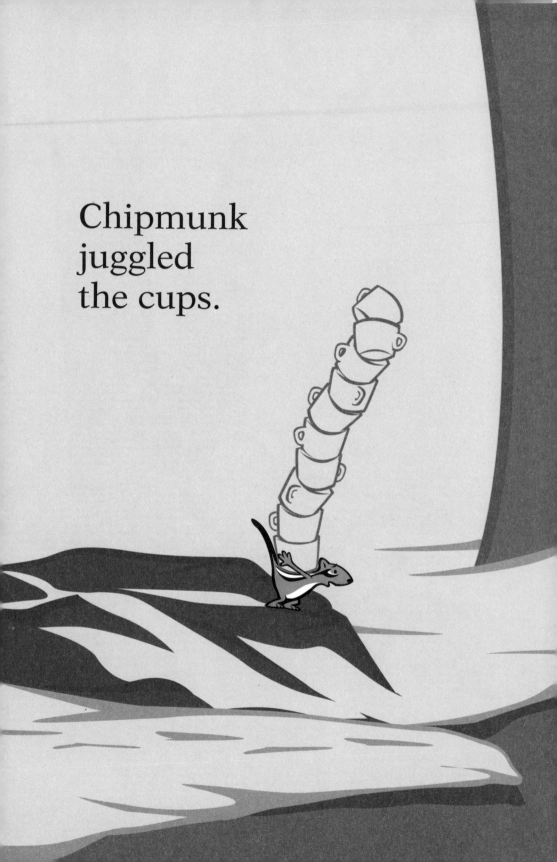

Fox made
the hot
chocolate.

The animals rolled . . .

and rolled

and rolled the snow.

Then they piled

and piled the snow.

Bear
attached
the branches.

Deer held the broom.

Mouse pushed
in the buttons.

Blue Jay tied the scarf.

Kitten
slid on the
mittens.

Squirrel added the acorns.

Rabbit put on the carrot.

Skunk placed the hat.

Chipmunk
passed out
the cups.

Fox
poured
the hot
chocolate.

They
raised
their
steaming
cups—

to toast
their new
friend.